THE FIRE STEALERS
A Hopi Story

ORIGINAL STORY BY MICHAEL LOMATUWAY'MA

COLLECTED AND TRANSLATED BY EKKEHART MALOTKI

ILLUSTRATED BY KEN GARY

Library of Congress Cataloging-in-Publication Data

Malotki, Ekkehart.
   The fire stealers : a Hopi story / adapted by Ekkehart Malotki from an
original story by Michael Lomatuway'ma ; illustrated by Ken Gary.
        p. cm.
Summary: Tells how several animals failed in their efforts to steal fire
for the Hopis, but eventually Vulture succeeded.
   ISBN 1-885772-13-0
1.   Hopi Indians--Folklore. 2.   Tales--Arizona. [1. Hopi
Indians--Folklore. 2. Indians of North America--Arizona--Folklore. 3.
Arizona--Folklore.]   I. Lomatuway'ma, Michael. II. Gary, Ken, ill. III.
Title.
   E99.H7M318 2003
   398.2'089'9745--dc21

                                                        2003003814

Design by Bob Jivanjee
Prepress: Ali Graphic Services Inc.
Printed in Hong Kong.

9 8 7 6 5 4 3 2 1

Kiva Publishing
Walnut, CA

About the Story and Illustrations

Story-telling was once an integral part of Hopi culture. It was practiced in the deep of winter, especially during the month known as Kyaamuya, roughly corresponding to parts of our December and January. Telling a story in summer, on the other hand, was strongly tabooed, and anyone doing so risked being bitten by a rattlesnake. In Third Mesa villages, stories always began with the word *aliksa'i* "listen," and usually ended formally with *pay yuk polo,* "and here the story ends." A good storyteller, with many tales, legends, and myths to relate, was described as a *tuwutsmoki,* literally a "story bag."

I originally published the present narrative, *Hin Hopiit Mooti Qööhit Haqamya* (How the Hopis First Got Fire) in Hopi Animal Tales (University of Nebraska Press, 1998), in both Hopi and English. I recorded it from Michael Lomatuway'ma, from the Third Mesa village of Hotevilla, and the English renderings were designed to strike a middle course between too close and too free a translation. Considered somewhat disjointed and formal in that format, the story was retitled *The Fire Stealers* and reworked to improve its narrative flow and its appeal to young readers. It remains, however, completely true to its Hopi origins in its core values and expressions. For all reworking suggestions I sincerely thank Diane Orr and Ken Gary.

This book would not have become a reality without the unique illustrations created by Ken Gary. Ken was inspired by ancient Pueblo kiva murals, particularly those at Pottery Mound in New Mexico, and at Awat'ovi and Kawaika-a in Arizona. Since stories such as this take place in what might be called mythological time, it was thought appropriate to create drawings reminiscent of the highly stylized, geometric, two dimensional, mythological motifs of these murals. No one knows what ancient Pueblo people actually looked like and exactly how they were dressed, but mural fragments and surviving bits of textiles, pottery, and other artifacts, along with knowledge of modern Hopi and Pueblo material and ritual culture, provide a tantalizing basis for an imaginative reconstruction such as this.

Aliksa'i (Listen!). Long ago when the Hopis came to this land, the nights were very cold and the people were freezing and miserable. They had no fire to keep warm by or to cook their food with.

In the mornings, when the Hopis looked east to greet the sun with a prayer, they saw smoke rising in the air. Somewhere fires were burning. The Hopi leaders gathered to discuss how they could get some of this fire for themselves and their people.

The Hopis ordered a strong young man to go and find the fire. He journeyed to the east, traveling by day and sleeping at night. It was bitter cold. Finally, he reached a village glowing with the light of fires. He saw people warming themselves by fires in their stone houses and he smelled the rich odors of cooking stew.

The young man returned home and told the leaders what he had found. After mulling over the news, they said, "We must get someone to steal fire for us."

The young man explained that no human being could ever steal a burning stick or hot coals from the village. There were too many people living there and they danced all night by the edge of the fire.

Also, there were guards stationed around the village, so no human could ever reach the plaza. The men thought and thought about who could carry out the task. In those days, the Hopi people were able to talk with animals, and each animal had special abilities. They thought maybe an animal could succeed where a human could not.

Finally, the Hopi leaders decided to ask Owl to help. Owl is a good scout and has extraordinary eyesight. Owl hooted loudly and agreed to the challenge.

Owl flew silently through the night to the village. As he approached the fire, the bright flames did something to his eyes. Owl was blinded, but still he tried to seize a firebrand. At sunrise he gave up. Hardly able to see in the daylight, the poor thing flew in circles, scared and lost. Finally, at nightfall, he regained his eyesight and returned to Hopiland without any fire. When he arrived, Owl told the leaders how he had been blinded by the flames. This is the reason owls see poorly in the brightness of the day and so much better at night.

The Hopis were more eager than ever to warm themselves by a fire. Again, they wondered who among the animals could carry out their request. The men talked and talked until they agreed on Gopher. After all, Gopher was accustomed to traveling underground and could probably sneak into the village. The men then carefully planned the route Gopher would tunnel and the exact place where he would pierce through the surface of the earth.

Gopher followed the leaders' plan and burrowed his way toward the village. Upon reaching his goal, he poked his head up. He was only a short distance from the fire. Nearby some women were grinding corn.

Gopher quickly grabbed a burning stick. Gripping the firebrand in his mouth, he rushed into his tunnel and hurried away. As he ran underground, smoke began to fill the tunnel. The cloud grew thicker and thicker until everything became black. Poor Gopher could not see anything, and he stumbled forward, bumping into roots and rocks. At last, he reached the tunnel entrance, but the firebrand was gone.

When the leader of the Hopis saw Gopher, he was disappointed and asked why he had returned empty-handed. Gopher answered, "Your plans were fine. But on the way back, the firebrand began smoking and smoldering. My tunnel turned completely black. I was coughing and tears were running from my eyes. I had to drop the firebrand. There was nothing else I could do. I'm afraid you'll have to find someone else." Then Gopher showed the men his tail. Only a tiny tip remained. The rest had been burned off. This is the reason gophers have such short tails.

Once more the men thought hard, desperate to find someone who could steal the fire. Then someone suggested Coyote. Coyote is constantly on the prowl and he's known to be a good thief. People don't even notice him whenever he takes something. Also, being a bit gullible, Coyote would no doubt quickly agree to go. So the Hopis sent a runner to Coyote's den to summon him.

Coyote agreed to assist the Hopis. He trotted to the village, quickly snatched up a firebrand and sneaked quietly away. Suddenly, however, the fire flamed up and Coyote howled as his entire pelt caught fire. Terrified, he dropped the firestick and ran back to his den. Because Coyote's pelt caught fire, all coyotes now have a yellowish-brown coat.

Once more the Hopis' plan had failed.

For the fourth time, the Hopis tried to decide who to ask for help. An old man recommended a big bird. Such a bird could snatch up a burning stick, fly high over the village and bring the fire to them. If its feathers got singed, the bird could drop the fire down to the ground. The leader agreed and exclaimed, "Vulture always circles the sky and is mighty and strong. He is certain to accomplish this feat." So the people bade Vulture to come.

Vulture replied bravely, "I will circle the village until I spot the flames you desire, then I will swoop down and seize a burning stick, unless the villagers harm or kill me."

"Well then, go in strength," the leader said as the big bird unfolded his wings and prepared to fly eastward. At nightfall, Vulture arrived at the brightly lit village. Far below, he spotted people dancing around fires. One fire was not quite ablaze, so Vulture swooped down and snatched a burning stick from it. Then, grasping the firebrand in his beak, he soared victoriously into the dark.

As Vulture winged westward, a strong breeze fanned the burning stick, sending flames higher and higher until they licked the bird's head. There was nothing the poor thing could do. By the time Vulture approached Hopiland, all the plumes on his head had caught fire. Frightened, the mighty bird dropped the stick and plunged to the ground.

Hopis who witnessed the terrible fall rushed to the bird. All of the glossy dark feathers on his head were still burning. With words of pity they began to rub his head to put out the flames. Unfortunately, they rubbed so hard that all his remaining head feathers came off and fell to the ground. For this reason vultures are now bald-headed.

The firebrand that had fallen lay nearby. When one of the Hopi leaders picked it up, first it sparked, then it burst into flames. He called everyone to come and celebrate Vulture's success, and leading a long procession, he carried the precious flame back home. Soon, every house in the village had some of the fire.

Thanks to Vulture, the Hopis now were warm and able to cook their meals. The Hopi leader told Vulture, "We're glad you stole the fire for us. We're overjoyed, but we cannot feed you our Hopi food. Instead, you can clean up our leftovers. Then it won't be so smelly around here anymore."

This is the reason why Vulture now mainly eats rotten things. He constantly circles the land, looking for decaying food, and in this manner cleans the earth.

This is how the Hopis finally acquired fire.

Pay yuk pölö. (And here the story ends).

Ekkehart Malotki is professor of languages at Northern Arizona University, where he has taught Latin, Hopi, and German since 1977. For over twenty-five years, his research has focused on preserving aspects of Hopi language and culture. In addition to numerous collections of Hopi narratives, he has published two children's books, *The Mouse Couple* and *The Magic Hummingbird*. He also contributed the majority of entries to the *Hopi Dictionary/Hopìikwa Lavàytutuveni*. Among his more recent works are *Hopi Stories of Witchcraft, Shamanism, and Magic*, jointly authored by his friend of many years, Ken Gary, and *Kokopelli: The Making of an Icon*. During the last ten years, his passion for photographing rock art of the American Southwest has resulted in two major publications: *Tapamveni: The Rock Art Galleries of Petrified Forest and Beyond* (with Pat McCreery) and *Stone Chisel and Yucca Brush: Colorado Plateau Rock Art* (with Donald E. Weaver, Jr.).

Ken Gary is an artist, writer, and craftsman who has been seriously studying American Indians since he was a young boy in a small town in Texas, reading everything he could find on the subject. When he got older he became especially interested in the people of the Southwest, particularly the Hopis and their ancestors. Eventually he was fortunate enough to have Hopi friends and to help write and illustrate such scholarly books as the *Hopi Dictionary*, published by the University of Arizona, and *Hopi Animal Tales*, by his good friend Ekkehart Malotki. This is the first time he has illustrated a children's book. He hopes it will inspire young readers to learn more about the ancient cultures of the Southwest, who have much to teach us about being human.

Phillips